To _____

Love _____

First published 1989 by Walker Books Ltd
87 Vauxhall Walk, London SE11 5HJ

This edition published 2003

2 4 6 8 10 9 7 5 3

This book has been typeset in New Century Schoolbook

Printed in Hong Kong

British Library Cataloguing in Publication Data:
a catalogue record for this book
is available from the British Library

ISBN 0-7445-5753-4

MY **DAD** IS
BRILLIANT

Nick Butterworth

WALKER BOOKS
AND SUBSIDIARIES

LONDON • BOSTON • SYDNEY

My dad is brilliant.

He's as strong as a gorilla ...

and he can run like a cheetah …

and he can play any instrument ...

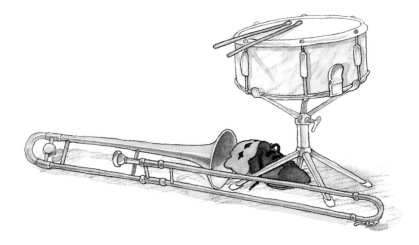

and he's a marvellous cook …

and he's fantastic
on roller skates …

and he's brilliant at
making things ...

and he can sing like a pop star ...

and he can juggle anything ...

and he's not a bit
frightened of the dark …

and he tells the funniest
jokes in the world.

It's great to have
a dad like mine.

It's brilliant!